What Are Some Forms of Energy?

HOUGHTON MIFFLIN HARCOURT

PHOTOGRAPHY CREDITS: COVER ©Reed Kaestner/Corbis; 3 (b) ©Herbert Kratky/Shutterstock; 5 (bg) ©Corbis; 7 (t) ©Tumar/Shutterstock; 8 (b) ©Darwin Dale/Photo Researchers, Inc.; 10 (bl) ©Eric Isselee/Shutterstock; 10 (br) ©Dorling Kindersley/Getty Images; 10 (bc) ©Getty Images; 11 (b) ©PhotoAlto/ Getty Images; 12 (bl) ©Rubberball/Getty Images; 13 (t) ©Reed Kaestner/ Corbis; 14 (b) ©Comstock/Getty Images; 15 (t) ©Microzoa; 16 (br) ©Kate Powers/Getty Images

Printed in China

ISBN: 978-0-544-07271-8

11 12 13 14 0940 20 19 18 17

4500693652   A B C D E F G

Be an Active Reader!

Look for each word in yellow along with its meaning.

energy	vibrate	shadow
potential energy	pitch	electrical energy
kinetic energy	reflect	heat
mechanical energy	absorb	temperature
sound	refract	

Underlined sentences answer these questions.

What is energy?

Is all energy the same?

What is sound energy?

How do we measure loudness?

How do we hear sounds?

What is pitch?

What is light energy?

Can light change direction?

Why do shadows form?

What is electrical energy?

What is heat?

What is energy?

It's busy at the swim meet! Many things are moving. Divers are stretching. Swimmers are kicking. Water is splashing. Diving boards are bending. All this movement takes energy. <u>Energy is the ability to do work, like making something move or change.</u>

You're about to turn the page. You'll need energy to do that. Moving or changing something takes energy.

It takes energy to move something. Where is energy at work at this swim meet?

Is all energy the same?

Not all energy is the same. Energy can be potential or kinetic. Potential energy is energy that's there but not being used. Kinetic energy is energy of motion. Objects that are moving have kinetic energy.

People and things can have both kinds of energy. Look at the diver. On the diving board, she has potential energy. As she begins to fall forward, she has kinetic energy, too. She has both. The total of an object's potential and kinetic energy is mechanical energy.

The diver stands on the board. She is ready to dive. What kind of energy does she have?

The diver jumps off the board. Her potential energy begins to turn into kinetic energy.

Climbing the ladder gives the diver potential energy. As she climbs higher, she stores more potential energy.

When the girl dives, she uses this potential energy. The potential energy changes into kinetic energy. It moves her downward.

What is sound energy?

Swim meets are noisy! People clap and cheer. Whistles blow. The meets have a lot of sound energy.

Sound is energy you can hear. You know that energy is the ability to make something move or change. An object makes sound when it vibrates. Vibrate means "move back and forth very quickly." The object might be a car horn or something as small as a mosquito.

The vibrations start the matter around them moving. These new movements spread in waves. Sound waves can travel through air, water, and solid things. You hear sound when the waves reach your ears.

Sound waves are vibrations that move outward from an object.

Sounds louder than 85 dB can hurt your ears. Which sounds at a swim meet might hurt your ears?

Sound	Decibels
Whistle	90
100 people clapping	80
A person cheering loudly	110

How do we measure loudness?

We can measure length in centimeters (cm). We can measure mass in kilograms (kg). We measure the loudness of sound in decibels (dB).

The table above shows the loudness of some sounds at a swim meet.

How do we hear sounds?

An object vibrates quickly. It starts the air around it vibrating. Sound waves spread out from the object. When the waves reach us, they make tiny bones in our ears vibrate. That is how we hear sounds.

Shake your hand back and forth quickly. You didn't hear any sound. That's because your hand didn't move quickly enough to make a sound that you could hear. People can hear only things that vibrate at least 20 times in a second.

A mosquito can move its wings about 600 times in a second. That's why you can hear it buzz!

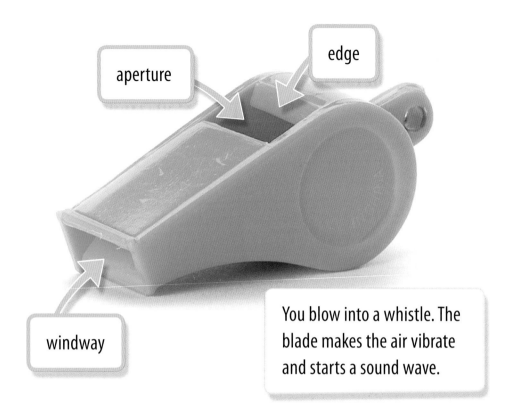

aperture

edge

windway

You blow into a whistle. The blade makes the air vibrate and starts a sound wave.

People blow whistles to begin swim meet races. There is a small blade inside a whistle. The air vibrates quickly when it moves across the blade. This vibration makes the whistling sound.

People also cheer at races. Feel your throat when you talk. You'll feel the vibrations that make the sound.

What is pitch?

Pitch is how high or low a note or sound is. When something vibrates quickly, it makes a sound that has a high pitch. When something vibrates slowly, it makes a sound that has a low pitch.

Your voice can get louder and higher when you get excited. That happens because the part of your throat that makes your voice vibrates faster. The faster vibrations make the pitch go up.

Size can also change pitch. Think of guitar strings. The bigger ones vibrate more slowly than smaller ones and have a lower pitch.

Which animal's sound has a high pitch?
Which animal's sound has a low pitch?

whale

lion

canary

What is light energy?

Light is a kind of energy. Like sound, light travels in waves. Light waves can move through empty space. They can also move through air, water, and glass. Light waves move in a straight line if nothing changes their path.

Light waves can also reflect, or bounce off, things like water and glass. Have you ever seen your face in a puddle? That happens because the light from your face bounces off the water back to you.

Water and other kinds of matter can also absorb, or take in, light. When you look down into deep water, you can't see to the bottom. The water absorbs the light.

You see your reflection when light from your face bounces back to you.

Can light change direction?

You learned that glass and water reflect light. Glass and water can also refract light. *Refract* means "to bend or change direction." For example, light can change direction when it moves from air to water.

Look at the picture of the children sitting by the pool. Light from the upper half of their legs went through air straight to the camera. Light from the lower half of their legs went through water first. As it moved from water to air, the light changed direction. See how this makes the lower half of the children's legs look as if they are not connected?

Refraction makes the bottom half of these legs look disconnected.

Why does the shadow have the shape of the swimmer?

Why do shadows form?

Look at the swimmer's shadow on the bottom of the pool. A shadow is a dark area behind an object that has blocked the light. Light moves in a straight line. So a shadow has the same shape as the object blocking the light.

What is electrical energy?

Electrical energy comes from tiny bits of matter called electrons. Electrons can have potential energy. Electrical energy can move through wires and do work.

We use electrical energy to power things. In your classroom, electrical energy makes lights work. At swim meets, it makes the microphone and the speakers work.

Electrical equipment should not be used close to water. Electrical energy can move through the water and hurt people.

Lightning is a huge burst of electrical energy.

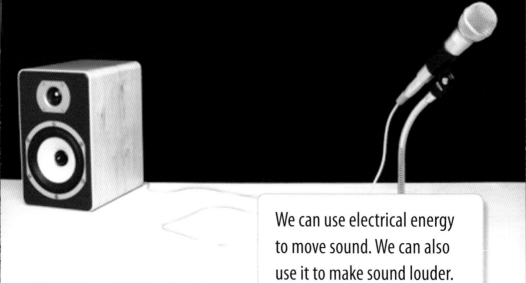

We can use electrical energy to move sound. We can also use it to make sound louder.

Electrical energy powers microphones and speakers. It also helps them work in another way. It carries sound between them.

Emile Berliner made the first microphone. He made it to use in telephones. A microphone turns sound energy into electrical energy. The electrical energy can travel through wires.

The part of a telephone you put to your ear is a small speaker. A speaker turns the electrical energy back into sound energy. Then you can hear it.

Some speakers make sound louder than it was before. People use this kind of speaker at sporting events.

What is heat?

Heat is the energy that comes from the movement of the tiny particles that make up matter. Heat moves from warmer objects to cooler objects. Think of a swimmer who has just come out of the pool. She wraps up in a towel that has been warmed by the sun. The heat energy moves from the warm towel to her cool body.

Heat moves from the towel to the girl's skin. Her skin gets warmer. The towel gets cooler.

Temperature is how hot or cold something is. Thermometers measure temperature. Some thermometers show how hot or cold it is outside. Maybe you've checked your body's temperature with a thermometer when you were sick.

There are two different ways of reading temperature on this thermometer. The numbers on the left show degrees Fahrenheit (°F). The numbers on the right show degrees Celsius (°C).

The reading on the left side is 73 °F. The reading on the right side is 23 °C. Both show the same level of heat energy.

Record Temperatures

Place a Celsius thermometer near a window that doesn't get much sunshine. For one week, check the temperature on the thermometer three times a day. Check in the morning. Check again at lunchtime. Then check just before you leave at the end of the day. Record each temperature in a table. Do the temperatures change? Do you see a pattern? Below your table, write your explanation for what you see.

Write about Safety

Choose one of the forms of energy you have learned about. What kinds of safety equipment do you need when you explore this form of energy? Why? Write your answers in a paragraph.

Glossary

absorb [ab·SAWRB] Take in by an object.

electrical energy [ee·LEK·tri·kuhl EN·er·jee] A form of energy that can move through wires. *Electrical energy travels through a wire to reach your television.*

energy [EN·er·jee] The ability to make something move or change. *It takes a lot of energy to run a race.*

heat [HEET] Energy that moves from warmer to cooler objects. *The heat from the fireplace warmed the girl's cold feet.*

kinetic energy [ki·NET·ik EN·er·jee] The energy of motion. *There is a lot of kinetic energy in a soccer game.*

mechanical energy [muh·KAN·i·kuhl EN·er·jee] The total potential and kinetic energy of an object.

pitch [PICH] How high or low a sound is. *A flute has a higher pitch than a tuba.*

potential energy [poh•TEN•shuhl EN•er•jee] Energy of position or condition. *As the roller coaster climbed the first hill, it gained potential energy.*

reflect [ri•FLEKT] To bounce off. *On a calm day, the lake will reflect the colors of the sunset.*

refract [ri•FRAKT] To bend light as it moves from one material to another. *Water refracts light, so it makes things look bent.*

shadow [SHAD•oh] A dark area that forms when an object blocks the path of light. *Shadow tag is a game that is played by stepping on a person's shadow.*

sound [SOWND] Energy that travels in waves you can hear. *The sound of the outdoor concert traveled across the lake.*

temperature [TEM•per•uh•cher] A measure of how hot or cold something is. *We couldn't eat the pizza because its temperature was too hot.*

vibrate [VY•brayt] To move back and forth very quickly. *Mosquitoes' wings vibrate and make a buzzing sound.*